ISBN 978-0-06-208086-8

10 11 12 13 14 LEO 10 9 8 7 6 5 4 3 2 1

Fancy NANCY

The Show Must Go On

by Jane O'Connor

cover illustration by Robin Preiss Glasser

interior illustrations by Ted Enik

HARPER
An Imprint of HarperCollinsPublishers

"Quiet, please," says Ms. Glass.

"I have an announcement."

(That means she has something

important to tell us.)

"The talent show is in a week."

Yay! Bree and I bump fists.

We have our act planned out already.

We will wear fancy circus costumes.

We will sing a song.

It is about daring girls on a trapeze.

Then Ms. Glass says,

"I am assigning partners."

Oh no!

That means we don't get to choose!

I am not assigned to Bree.

I am assigned to Lionel.

He is very shy.

I hardly know him.

Ms. Glass wants us

to brainstorm with our partner.

That means to talk over ideas.

So I ask Lionel,

"Do you like to sing?"

He says no.

He does not like to dance

or tell jokes.

He can wiggle his ears.

He can crack his fingers.

He can balance a spoon on his nose.

"Very cool," I say.

"But I can't do those things.

We need to perform together."

(Perform is a fancy word for act.)

That night I say,

"Bree and Yoko are partners.

They will do a fan dance

and wear kimonos."

(I explain that a kimono

is a fancy Japanese robe.)

"Lionel and I
can't think of anything to do."
I sigh a deep sigh.
"And now I won't get to wear
my circus costume."

Mom says, "Ask Lionel over.

Get to know each other.

It will help you plan an act."

On Saturday I ask Lionel over.

But his mom can't drop him off.

So Dad drives me to Lionel's house.

Ooh la la! It is very fancy.

It is almost a mansion.

Lionel's room is huge.

(Huge is much bigger than big.)

There are lots of toy lions.

"Oh! I get it!" I say.

"You like lions

because your name is Lionel."

I pick up a little glass lion.

"This is adorable," I say.

I tell him I like fancy words.

And adorable is fancy for cute.

Lionel shows me a lion mask.

"Wow," I say. "It's great!"

He puts on the mask.

"Grrr," Lionel says, and chases me.

We race all over his house.

"Help! Help!" I yell.

Later we have snacks.

"You're a great lion," I tell Lionel.

Then I get an extremely great idea!

"Let's do a circus act.

You can be the lion.

I can be the lion tamer.

I already have a costume."

Lionel likes the idea. Yay!

The next week we get together

many times to rehearse.

(That's a fancy word for practice.)

Still, we are nervous
on the day of the show.
We hear Ms. Glass announce,
"Here is Lady Lulubell
and the man-eating lion!"

The curtain opens.

Lionel jumps through the hoop.

Lionel walks on a pretend tightrope.

Then he roars and chases me.

"Don't eat me!" I cry.

"Eat this instead!"

I hand Lionel a huge lollipop.

He starts licking it and purring.

Then I curtsy and he bows.

Our act is over.

There is a lot of applause!

(That's a fancy word for clapping.)

I hear my dad shout, "Bravo!"

We all go out for ice cream.

I give Lionel a clay lion I made.

And guess what?

He teaches me

to balance a spoon on my nose!

Fancy Nancy's Fancy Words

These are the fancy words in this book:

Adorable—cute

Announcement—something important to tell

Applause—clapping

Assign—to choose something for someone else

Brainstorm—to talk over lots of ideas

Bravo—way to go!

Kimono—fancy Japanese robe

Mansion—a very fancy house

Perform—to act (or dance or sing)

Rehearse—to practice